# THE
# FAIRY
# ATLAS

LAURENCE KING

First published in Great Britain in 2022
by Laurence King Publishing

Text © 2022 Anna Claybourne
Illustrations © 2022 Miren Asiain Lora, c/o Phileas Fogg Agency

A catalog record for this book is available
from the British Library

ISBN: 978-1-9139-4728-6

MIX
Paper from
responsible sources
FSC® C104740

10 9 8 7 6 5 4 3 2 1

Printed and bound in China

Laurence King Publishing
An imprint of
Hachette Children's Group
Part of Hodder and Stoughton
Carmelite House
50 Victoria Embankment
London EC4Y 0DZ

An Hachette UK Company
www.hachette.co.uk
www.hachettechildrens.co.uk
www.laurenceking.com

Laurence King Publishing is committed to
ethical and sustainable production.
We are proud participants in The Book Chain Project ®
bookchainproject.com

BOOK
CHAIN
PROJECT

*The stories and information in this book come from the
ancient traditional tales and folklore of many peoples
around the world. In each case, the author has chosen
one retelling, although there may be many different
versions of each story or tradition.*

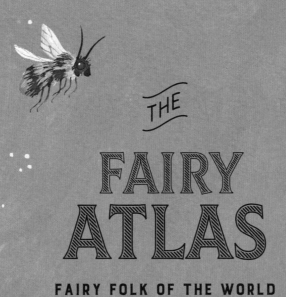

# THE
# FAIRY
# ATLAS

## FAIRY FOLK OF THE WORLD

WORDS BY
ANNA CLAYBOURNE

ILLUSTRATIONS BY
MIREN ASIAIN LORA

# CONTENTS

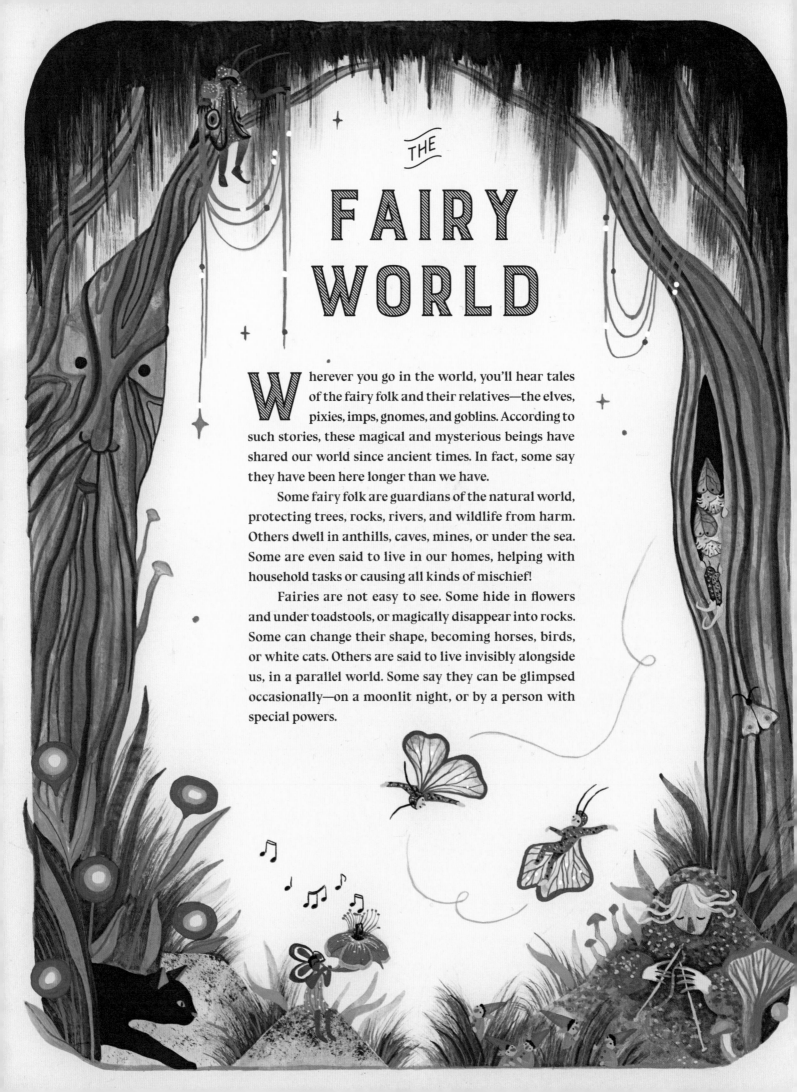

# THE FAIRY WORLD

**W**herever you go in the world, you'll hear tales of the fairy folk and their relatives—the elves, pixies, imps, gnomes, and goblins. According to such stories, these magical and mysterious beings have shared our world since ancient times. In fact, some say they have been here longer than we have.

Some fairy folk are guardians of the natural world, protecting trees, rocks, rivers, and wildlife from harm. Others dwell in anthills, caves, mines, or under the sea. Some are even said to live in our homes, helping with household tasks or causing all kinds of mischief!

Fairies are not easy to see. Some hide in flowers and under toadstools, or magically disappear into rocks. Some can change their shape, becoming horses, birds, or white cats. Others are said to live invisibly alongside us, in a parallel world. Some say they can be glimpsed occasionally—on a moonlit night, or by a person with special powers.

# WHAT IS A FAIRY?

You may think of fairies as small, winged creatures, glowing with light as they flit through the air. Some fairies do fit this description —but many more do not. While they can be little—sometimes even tinier than ants—there are fairy folk that can grow as big as a human. Some can fly, but many gnomes and goblins walk on the ground. They may be bad-tempered and frightening to look at.

# TAKE CARE!

Although fairies can be helpful and kind, never forget that they have magical powers. Treat them well and they may bring you good luck, share their knowledge, or complete household tasks. Kind fairies will rescue lost children, grant your wishes, or help your garden grow. But people who annoy fairy folk, or tangle with a dangerous fairy, may find that strange things start to happen. Objects go missing, odd noises are heard in the night, or people end up hopelessly lost in the woods. Always treat the natural world with respect and tread lightly, for a fairy may be nearby ...

# EUROPE

We begin in Europe, home to a treasure trove of traditional tales and ancient places—and a cornucopia of fairy creatures.

Many of Europe's fairies are found living alongside humans. Across the northern lands of this continent, barely a household is without its own Brownie, Nisse, or Tomte. These fairy helpers will finish off the housework and guard the home, if you treat them with respect. They are said to play tricks on you if you don't!

Homes are not the only places where you'll find fairies in this folklore-filled continent. They flit through forests, guard trees and wild animals, and sprinkle gold into rivers. They dwell in fairy castles high in the mountains, inside rocks and caves, and even underground. Fairy folk roam the moors, dance in the moonlight, and inhabit the great monuments and stone circles that the people of these lands built long ago.

*ICELAND*

Any rock or crag could be home to the hidden **HULDUFÓLK**

*SCOTLAND*

Home of the friendly household **BROWNIES**

Find the silvery, human-sized **AOS SÍ** here

*IRELAND*

Beware the tricks of the famous fairy **PUCK**

*ENGLAND*

The **PIXIES** of Cornwall may lead you far from the beaten track

Need a job done? Ask the hardworking **GALTZAGORRI**

*SPAIN*

SWEDEN

FINLAND

Nature-guarding **HALTIJAS** inhabit trees, rocks, and rivers

RUSSIA

NORWAY

**NISSE** (known as Tomte in Sweden) are housework-loving gnomes

DENMARK

POLAND

GERMANY

You might catch a glimpse of the beautiful **TÜNDÉR** here

Wild, green **MOOSLEUTE** live among the tree roots

The mischievous **LUTIN** has a thousand tricks to play

FRANCE

SLOVENIA

HUNGARY

The ghostly **VILAS** dance by night in the forest glades

BULGARIA

ITALY

A banging noise at home means a **MAZZAMURELLO** is in residence

## PUCK
### ENGLAND

England is full of enchanted places, with names such as Fairyhill, Fairy Dell, and Fairy Holes Cave. Fairies have always been important in this ancient land. The most famous of them all is Puck, or Robin Goodfellow. He's a nature spirit, at home in the forest, but he also visits people's homes. At night, this terrible trickster may blow out candles, tug blankets off beds, or plant a spooky dream in a sleeping person's head. But leave him a drink of milk and a piece of bread, and he might sweep the house clean for you, or finish your sewing, in the tiniest of fairy stitches.

## BROWNIE
### SCOTLAND

In Scottish folklore, every large house or farm was said to have its own household fairy, called a Brownie (or Broonie). Small, quiet, and dressed in brown rags, a Brownie will do all kinds of work—such as plowing a field overnight, churning butter, or cleaning the house—in return for a simple bowl of cream or porridge. Brownies are very proud and will be insulted if you leave them any other payment. Should you dare to give a Brownie clothes to replace his rags, he'll be so offended he'll leave your home, never to be seen again.

## AOS SÍ
### IRELAND

Although they live alongside humans, the Aos Sí are rarely seen. They protect their ancient burial mounds, as well as nearby trees, hills, and lakes. You may glimpse the Aos Sí when they visit our world at dawn or dusk. A small whirlwind passing by, or a sound like humming bees, could reveal their presence. Unlike many fairies, the Aos Sí are tall, and shine with silvery light. To show them respect, people often call them "the good neighbors" or "the shining folk." Befriend these fairies, and they may heal you when you are sick, or teach you magical metalwork, weaving, or dancing skills.

# PIXIES

## A MYSTERIOUS DISAPPEARANCE

### CORNWALL

Pixies, also called Piskies, are the fairies of Cornwall and southwestern England. They are small and mischievous, and love to play and dance. Though mostly harmless, they sometimes ride humans' horses at night, tangling up their manes. There are also many local tales of Pixies leading people astray on moors and in forests.

One such story tells of a boy from the village of St. Allen, who went to pick flowers in the woods near his house. His mother clearly saw him there, but when she looked a second time, he was gone. She went to search for him, and he was nowhere to be found. For two days and nights, the villagers looked everywhere for the boy. Then, on the third day, they found him asleep on a pile of ferns, in the exact same place he had vanished from.

When he woke up, the boy had no idea how long he had been missing. He said he had heard and followed a beautiful song in the woods. Coming to the edge of a lake, he saw that night had fallen, and the sky seemed to be full of huge, bright stars. Then he realized that they were not stars, but Pixies. They led him into their underground home, which was like a palace, its ceiling strung with jewels. The Pixies gave him cakes and honey and sang to him until he fell asleep. The next thing he knew, he was waking up among the ferns, with the villagers around him.

They say that the boy lived a long, happy life, blessed by his encounter. But however hard he tried, he could never remember the beautiful tune of the Pixies' magical music.

## NISSE
### NORWAY, DENMARK, AND SWEDEN

The Nisse (known as a Tomte in Sweden) is a gnomelike creature who resembles a tiny old man. Despite his small size, a Nisse is incredibly strong and skilled in toolmaking, craftwork, and magic. He is rarely seen because he can make himself invisible. A Nisse may live on a farm and help the farmer, requiring only a bowl of porridge once a year. You can recognize a farm with a Nisse by its beautifully groomed horses (the Nisse's favorite animal). Make sure you never annoy a Nisse by treating animals badly—he may whack you on the head from behind, or even give you a nasty bite!

## HALTIJAS AND THE FAIRY TREE
### FINLAND

In Finland, Haltijas, or "holders," are elf-like fairy guardians. There are many different types of Haltija, and they protect the forests, lakes, streams, villages, and farms. Each person has their very own Haltija too, who guards and looks after them. Even trees have their own special Haltijas, and traditionally families had a Haltijapuu, or Fairy Tree, in their garden. On special occasions, the old custom is to leave food and gifts under the tree for the Haltija who lives there, to thank it for guarding the household.

## HULDUFÓLK
### ICELAND

These Icelandic elves are said to live in rocks and crags. Their name means "hidden people," as you can only see these magical beings if they choose to show themselves—or if you have a special ability. The Huldufólk look similar to humans but live for longer. Some people put small shelters for the Huldufólk in their gardens, or candles in their windows to light the way on New Year's Eve, when the Huldufólk are said to move home. Icelandic folklore warns against throwing stones, in case you accidentally hit one of the Huldufólk.

## MOOSLEUTE
### GERMANY

The forests of Bavaria, southeastern Germany, are home to the tiny Moosleute or Moss Folk. These timid forest fairies protect the trees and weave the soft moss that covers the tree roots and rocks. They wear clothes of moss, and look like tiny trees themselves, with gnarled hands and long gray hair, like lichen. When household items go missing in this part of the world, it's said that they must have been borrowed by a Moss Woman. In return, she will teach humans how to cure illnesses, using the herbs of the forest.

## MAZZAMURELLO
### ITALY

If you hear a strange knocking and banging on the walls of a house in Italy, it might have a Mazzamurello. This creature is often described as a nature elf or goblin, living in the mountains or hiding in trees—but he will sometimes move into a human home. It's said that he bangs on the walls to send the homeowners a message: either there is hidden treasure somewhere on the property, or someone in the house is in great danger.

## LUTIN
### FRANCE

This troublesome fairy of northern France is a shapeshifter, and can change itself into any animal— rabbit, dog, cat, or mouse. If you see a cat that's completely white all over, it could well be a Lutin in disguise. A Lutin may also turn itself into a horse, complete with a saddle and ready to ride. But if anyone rides it, it will run like the wind, carrying them far away. Lutins play other tricks too, making holes in fishing nets, tangling up people's hair while they sleep, or filling their shoes with stones. If you don't want a Lutin around, simply sprinkle salt in the doorway—they hate salt and will not step over it.

# GALTZAGORRI

## TOO MUCH HELP IS WORSE THAN NONE AT ALL!

### BASQUE COUNTRY SPAIN

The Basque Country of northern Spain is home to imp-like fairies called the Galtzagorri, meaning "red pants." These clever creatures will take on any task. However, this isn't always as helpful as it might seem.

According to an old story, there once lived a man who was no good at anything. If he planted vegetables, they died. If he mended a fence, it broke again. The man was fed up, so he asked a wise old woman what to do. She told him to buy some Galtzagorri, who would change his life.

The man bought a box of four Galtzagorri. He opened it, and out jumped the little imps, shouting, "What do you want us to do?" The man was delighted. He asked the Galtzagorri to plow his field and plant seeds. They did it in minutes. He asked them to feed and milk his cow. It was done in a flash. The Galtzagorri did every task he gave them—collecting firewood, cooking dinner, mending the roof, pruning the apple tree, making cheese—and each time they completed a task, they flew around the man's head, asking, "What do you want us to do now?"

There was nothing more to do, but the Galtzagorri wanted more tasks, so they began to undo all the work they had already done. Desperate to stop them, the man gave the Galtzagorri a sieve. "Fetch me some water in this!" he said. That would keep them busy!

But when the Galtzagorri tried to fill the sieve and failed, they were angry. "You have given us an impossible task!" they shouted. "We're leaving! You'll never see us again!" And with that, they disappeared.

The man breathed a sigh of relief. From that day on he was happy to work hard and do all his tasks properly himself. His life had changed, just as the wise old woman had said!

# TÜNDÉR
## HUNGARY

The Tündér are powerful female fairies of Hungary. They protect orphans and help the poor by giving them pearls. When they brush their long golden hair, they scatter gold into rivers and streams. They wear white and can fly, taking the form of a swan. Some say the Tündér used to live among people, but left long ago as they do not like the modern world. They retreated to their mountaintop palaces, which have beautiful gardens, each with a golden, spinning summerhouse. By moonlight, the Tündér come out to dance, and may sometimes visit human gardens, too, where they water and care for their favorite flowers.

# VILA
## BULGARIA, SLOVENIA, AND OTHER PARTS OF EASTERN EUROPE

Among the forests, lakes, and wild places of Eastern Europe, you'll hear tales of the Vilas: enchanting, ghostlike fairies who are beautiful, yet frightening. At night, Vilas come out to dance together in a circle, their long white robes and dresses billowing in the darkness. It's an amazing sight, but beware: Vilas do not like to be watched. If a young man sees a Vila dancing, she may curse him, making him fall in love with her forever. Or, even worse, she might cast a spell, forcing him to dance all night until he falls down dead.

# MEET THE FAIRY FOLK

**D**o you imagine fairies as tiny, magical creatures with shimmering wings and a suit of leaves, dwelling among forest flowers? You'll find this type of fairy in many stories, but fairy folk come in other forms, too. They may be old or young, female or male, small or human-sized, beautiful . . . or not so beautiful. Some flutter on gossamer wings, but others travel by shape-shifting into different animals, or walk on the ground just as humans do.

## ONE OR MANY?

According to fairy experts, fairies can be "solitary" or "trooping." Trooping fairies appear in groups, holding parties or processions, while solitary fairies live alone.

The Tylwyth Teg or "fair folk" of Wales are trooping fairies. They like to play music together and dance in a circle, led by a fairy king called Gwyn ap Nudd.

The Domovoy house elves of Ukraine are solitary fairies. If you have a Domovoy in your house or farm, he will be the only one you ever see.

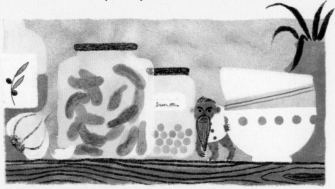

## GOOD OR BAD?

Are fairies good or bad? Like people, they can be both. Most helpful fairies, elves, and gnomes like to be treated with respect. If you upset them, or damage the forest, lake, or other place they guard, they may cast an unpleasant spell on you.

However, some are purely good, like the Zână of Romania, a kind of forest fairy godmother. She guides people lost in the woods to safety, and blesses babies when they are born.

Meanwhile, some are just scary, such as the Hantu Kayu of Malaysia. These "tree ghosts" are said to bring sickness or bad luck upon anyone who enters the forest.

# A GUIDE TO FAIRY FOLK

There are countless kinds of fairy folk, but they fall into several main groups or types.

## FAIRY
Beautiful, magical beings, true fairies are usually small, and often able to fly.

## ELF
Elves are more humanlike than true fairies (though they often have pointed ears).

## IMP
These small creatures are usually mischievous, and sometimes dangerous.

## BROWNIE
These helpful, scruffy, solitary fairies live in homes and do chores in return for food.

## PIXIE
These mischievous fairies dwell outdoors on moors or in ancient monuments.

## GNOME
Gnomes look just like tiny humans and live in forests, gardens, or mountains.

## GOBLIN
These small, magical creatures may steal things, spread bad luck, or harm people.

## SPRITES AND SPIRITS
The most ethereal and delicate of fairies, sprites have no solid form and may be invisible.

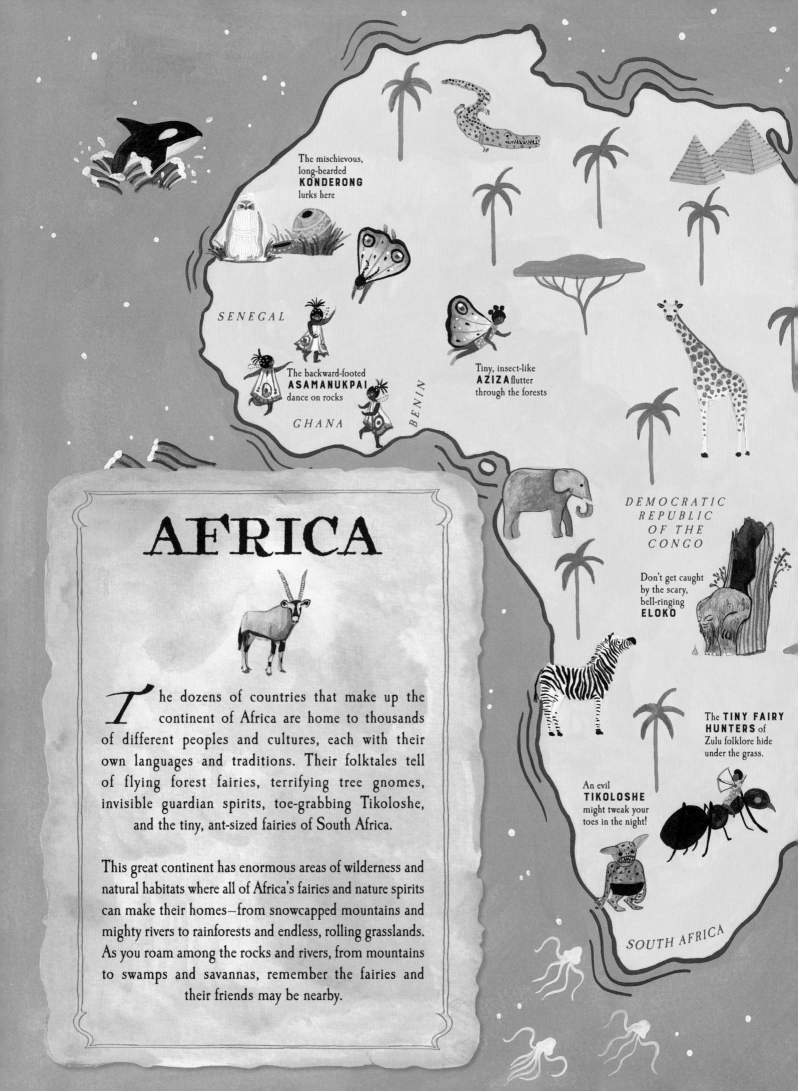

The mischievous, long-bearded **KONDERONG** lurks here

*SENEGAL*

The backward-footed **ASAMANUKPAI** dance on rocks

*GHANA*

*BENIN*

Tiny, insect-like **AZIZA** flutter through the forests

# AFRICA

The dozens of countries that make up the continent of Africa are home to thousands of different peoples and cultures, each with their own languages and traditions. Their folktales tell of flying forest fairies, terrifying tree gnomes, invisible guardian spirits, toe-grabbing Tikoloshe, and the tiny, ant-sized fairies of South Africa.

This great continent has enormous areas of wilderness and natural habitats where all of Africa's fairies and nature spirits can make their homes—from snowcapped mountains and mighty rivers to rainforests and endless, rolling grasslands. As you roam among the rocks and rivers, from mountains to swamps and savannas, remember the fairies and their friends may be nearby.

*DEMOCRATIC REPUBLIC OF THE CONGO*

Don't get caught by the scary, bell-ringing **ELOKO**

The **TINY FAIRY HUNTERS** of Zulu folklore hide under the grass.

An evil **TIKOLOSHE** might tweak your toes in the night!

*SOUTH AFRICA*

## ELOKO
### CONGO RIVER RAINFORESTS

In the jungles surrounding Central Africa's Congo River, beware of the Eloko, a frightening gnome who searches for humans to eat. These dangerous creatures, said to be the spirits of vengeful ancestors, live inside tree trunks. Grass grows all over their bodies in the place of hair and their eyes glow a fiery red. If their sensitive noses sniff out humans, they ring a tiny bell. Any person who hears the bell's tinkling sound falls under a deadly magical spell, which makes them willingly give themselves to an Eloko to be eaten.

## AZIZA
### BENIN

The people of Benin, West Africa, have legends about little forest fairies with beautiful butterfly-like wings, called the Aziza. They live in kapok trees or anthills, and they are kind, helpful, and caring. It's said they are the souls of the trees, in fairy form. Long ago, the Aziza appeared to the first people and showed them how to use plants as medicines, and how to make fire. Some say that when humans learned how helpful the Aziza were, they tried to find them to ask for more knowledge. But the shy Aziza retreated deeper into the jungle, which is why they are so hard to find today.

## KONDERONG
### WEST AFRICA

In the Wolof culture of West Africa, Konderong are small gnomes with back-to-front feet. They wear their long white beards wrapped around their bodies like clothes. They are invisible to most humans, but a few people with special powers can see them. Konderong are mischievous and mean. When someone is carrying a heavy load on their head, a Konderong may make it impossible for them to put it down. They are said to turn people blind so that they get lost, and even kidnap small children. However, there's a silver lining—if you manage to steal a Konderong's calabash, or water pot, its magic will make all your wishes come true.

## ASAMANUKPAI
### GHANA

The Asamanukpai are fairy folk of Ghana who, like the Konderong, have backward-facing feet. Despite this, they love to dance, especially on large rocks that stick up out of the ground. These rocks look shiny and polished, and sometimes have holes worn into them, which is the result of the Asamanukpai dancing on them for so long. If you go near these places, it's wise to take a gift of fruit and a pan or bowl of water. The Asamanukpai will use the water to bathe in. In return, they may squeeze magical plant juice into your eyes, allowing you to read the thoughts of others, and see into the future.

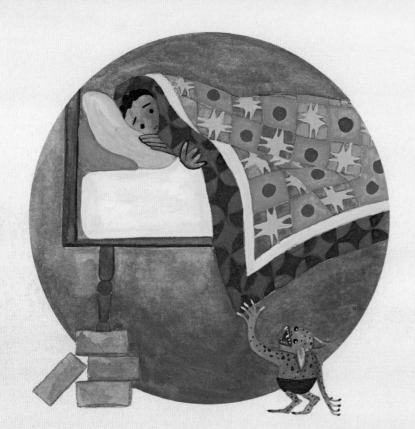

# TIKOLOSHE
## SOUTH AFRICA

When you go to bed, make sure there isn't a Tikoloshe around. In South African Zulu folklore, people can summon this horrible gremlin-like creature to give their enemies a fright. It creeps into people's bedrooms at night and disturbs their sleep by poking them, invading their dreams, or even grabbing and biting their toes! Luckily, however, a Tikoloshe is very small—so you can protect yourself by putting bricks under the legs of your bed to raise it up.

# TINY FAIRY HUNTERS
## SOUTH AFRICA

Zulu folktales tell of a group of extremely small fairy hunters. Fairies are usually small, but these fairies are minuscule! They are tiny enough to hide under blades of grass, ride on the backs of ants, and shelter in anthills. Most people cannot see them—only young children, pregnant women, and those with magical powers. When a woman is expecting a baby, she will see male fairies if she's having a boy and female fairies if it's a girl.

The tiny fairies are shy, and usually harmless. But they hate being reminded about how small they are. For this reason, if you spot one, it's a good idea to say "I saw you!" and remark on how large and noticeable they are. If you offend the fairies—or even worse, step on one—they will shoot you painfully in the foot with their tiny arrows. Although small, these poison-tipped arrows can be deadly.

# FAIRY LORE

There may be thousands of types of fairy folk around the world, but they often have similar abilities and habits. Learning a little fairy lore—knowledge of fairy traditions and fairy ways—will help you understand the fairies better, and avoid upsetting them, wherever your adventures may take you.

## FAIRY FLIGHT

Only true fairies have wings. Their relatives, including elves, gnomes, and Brownies, more often walk on two feet. A true fairy is an airy creature, who weighs almost nothing, and can dart around wherever they wish. While some fairies have butterfly-like wings, others can fly without them!

## FAIRY GOLD

There are many stories of humans stealing gold from fairies or receiving fairy gold as payment for a favor. In Irish folktales, Leprechauns are small fairies who keep pots of gold at the end of rainbows. If you catch a Leprechaun, he may give you the gold in exchange for his freedom. However, fairy gold is not always reliable. The next time you look at it, it might have turned into leaves, stones, little cakes, or even toadstools.

## CHANGELINGS

Around the world, there are stories of fairies who kidnap human children—sometimes replacing them with a fairy baby, or "changeling." Despite their magical powers, fairies are often said to be jealous of the beautiful, chubby babies of humans, and long to take and keep them. Luckily, however, the spell can be undone. If you manage to make the changeling baby laugh, it will vanish, and the human baby will be returned.

# FAIRY POWERS

Fairies and their relatives use magic in many ways. Among their magical powers, these are the most common.

## CASTING SPELLS

Fairy spells can make objects invisible, change the weather, make people fall in love, or–in the case of bad or angry fairies–cause disease and disaster.

## SUPER-SPEED

Fairy folk are fast workers. They can plow a field or tidy a house in an instant, or zoom around the world at lightning speed.

## WISDOM

Some kinds of fairies know how to make medicines, find the way through a forest, or talk to the animals. If you're lucky, they may teach you, too.

## INVISIBILITY

There's a reason you don't see fairies everywhere–their powers of invisibility! In fact, most fairies only appear to humans very rarely.

## LUMINESCENCE

Fairies often glow with light, especially when flying by night. You might mistake them for fireflies or stars.

## SHAPE-SHIFTING

A great many fairies can change their shape, usually into animals. An animal that is pure white all over could actually be a fairy.

## BEFRIENDING FAIRIES

Most fairies are harmless, as long as you treat them kindly. Behave respectfully in areas where fairies may be living, such as forests and other wild areas and around stone circles and other ancient monuments. You can even create little houses and place them in your garden for fairies to shelter in, or leave out gifts of their favorite food, such as cream, butter, milk, and porridge. If you treat them well, they may even start to leave little gifts for you at your door.

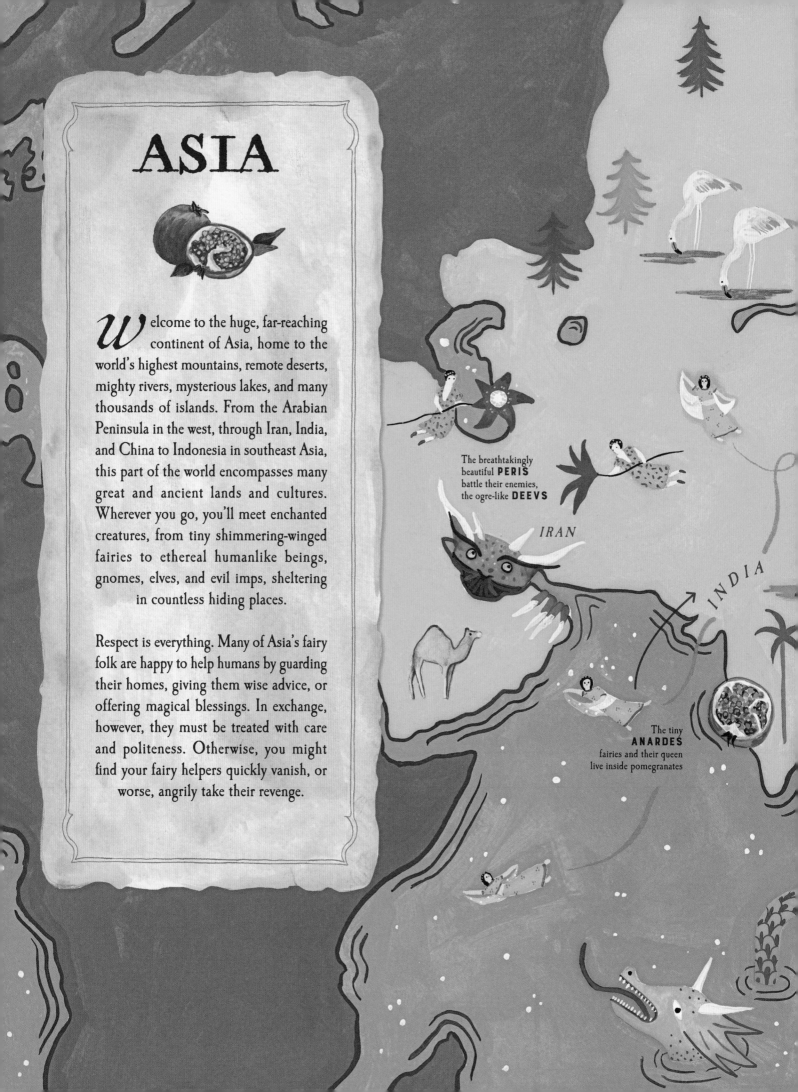

# ASIA

*W*elcome to the huge, far-reaching continent of Asia, home to the world's highest mountains, remote deserts, mighty rivers, mysterious lakes, and many thousands of islands. From the Arabian Peninsula in the west, through Iran, India, and China to Indonesia in southeast Asia, this part of the world encompasses many great and ancient lands and cultures. Wherever you go, you'll meet enchanted creatures, from tiny shimmering-winged fairies to ethereal humanlike beings, gnomes, elves, and evil imps, sheltering in countless hiding places.

Respect is everything. Many of Asia's fairy folk are happy to help humans by guarding their homes, giving them wise advice, or offering magical blessings. In exchange, however, they must be treated with care and politeness. Otherwise, you might find your fairy helpers quickly vanish, or worse, angrily take their revenge.

The breathtakingly beautiful **PERIS** battle their enemies, the ogre-like **DEEVS**

*IRAN*

*INDIA*

The tiny **ANARDES** fairies and their queen live inside pomegranates

The Jade Emperor's fairy princess daughter visits her beloved human in the tale of **TIAN XIAN PEI**

Beware the dreadful **MOKSIN TONGBOP** who spread diseases and try to sneak into houses

The **KORPOKKUR** live under the leaves of the butterbur plant

CHINA

KOREA

JAPAN

Don't tread on **NUNO SA PUNSO**, the "Grandpa of the Mound"

Look out for the handsome, glowing **TAMAWO**, who seeks a human wife

Home of helpful guardian elves, the **MRENH GONGVEAL**

CAMBODIA

Insect-winged **DAYAMDAM** fairies protect the trees and their fruits

The human-sized, misty-white **ORANG BUNIAN** live in forests and mountains

MALAYSIA

PHILIPPINES

INDONESIA

# KORPOKKUR

## THE FAIRIES WHO DISAPPEARED

### HOKKAIDO
### NORTHERN JAPAN

The Korpokkur are nature fairies of northern Japan, home of the ancient Ainu culture. Their name means "people who live under the butterbur." They are so small that they use the leaves of the butterbur plant to make roofs for their huts. They are extremely fast and nimble, and excellent at fishing, pottery, and toolmaking.

Long ago, so they say, the humans and the Korpokkur were good friends, even trading with each other. The Korpokkur were very shy and hated being looked at, so they would leave fresh fish outside the humans' homes at night, and in exchange, the humans left their own treasures there for the fairies to collect. People only ever caught a brief glimpse of the Korpokkur as they swiftly darted away.

One day, a nosy man decided to get a better look at the mysterious fairies. When night fell, he waited by his window until he heard the Korpokkur outside. Quickly he grabbed one by the arm and pulled it into his house to look at it by lamplight. He saw that he had caught a tiny, beautiful Korpokkur woman. She was furious at his behavior and demanded to be released. The man let her go, but from that day on, the Korpokkur went into hiding. They have never been seen since—though you might sometimes still come across their little huts and tools in the forest.

# FAIRIES OF THE PHILIPPINES

## NUNO SA PUNSO

Take care as you stroll in the forests of the Philippines, making sure you don't step on an ant's nest or a mushroom mound. It could be home to a small, grumpy Nuno sa Punso, or "Grandpa of the mound," who hates it when people disturb his home. If you accidentally tread on it or kick it, he'll cast a curse on you, giving you swollen feet, aches and pains, or even a hairy back! To keep the Nuno happy, always walk carefully around the mound, and call out "Tabi-tabi po" or "Excuse me!" as politely as you can.

## DAYAMDAM

These tiny, insect-sized forest fairies live in trees. They wear clothes and hats made of leaves, and play among the branches with the bees. Each Dayamdam guards its tree against danger. If you want to pick fruit or flowers from a tree, you must warn the Dayamdam first, and ask it not to get angry.

## TAMAWO

Some fairies, such as the Tamawo, are not tiny—they're at least as tall as humans. They're hard to see, however, because they live in a parallel world, invisible to human eyes. Occasionally, though, a Tamawo will appear and try to lure a female human to his own world to be his wife. Almost always male, the Tamawo are stunningly handsome with pale, glowing skin, hair, and eyes. They wear a golden crown and have golden fangs and claws.

## PERIS AND DEEVS
### IRAN

In ancient Persian folklore, Peris are delicate, winged creatures, glowing with shimmering, multicolored light. They do not eat food, instead surviving merely on the aroma of exquisite perfumes. Peris are kind and helpful to humans and represent the forces of good. In their own fairy world of Jinnestan, they must constantly wage war against the evil Deevs—giant, hairy ogres with terrifying tusks and snakes for hair. Many tales tell of Deevs capturing a Peri and shutting her in a cage that is left hanging from a tall treetop. The other Peris take perfume to feed their friend until she is able to escape.

## MRENH GONGVEAL
### CAMBODIA

In Cambodia, you'll often see little baskets hanging outside houses. In each basket is a little house and a selection of new, tiny clothes. This is an offering to the Mrenh Gongveal. Adults can't see them, but it's said that some children can. These wise little elves can be mischievous, but they also look after all kinds of things, including animals, places, and people. If they accept your gifts and decide to help you, you might hear them whispering advice in your ear, or receive a visit from them in a dream.

## ANARDES
### INDIA

A Gujarati folktale from western India tells of Prince Rupsinh, who longs to marry the Queen of the Anardes, magical fairies who live inside pomegranate fruits. With the help of a wise old hermit, Rupsinh finds the home of the Anardes in a pomegranate orchard, and watches as the fruits open and the tiny fairies come out to dance. As the hermit has instructed him, he picks the largest pomegranate, containing the fairy queen herself, and she becomes his wife.

# TIAN XIAN PEI
## CHINA

The story of Tian Xian Pei, or the "Fairy Couple," is known throughout China. The all-powerful Jade Emperor had seven fairy daughters. They left their father's magical kingdom to travel to the human world. There they met a kind cowherd, Dong Yong, who lived in poverty after paying for his father's funeral. The youngest fairy fell in love with him, and her sisters helped her weave cloth to pay off Dong Yong's debts, so that they could marry. But the Jade Emperor would not agree to the marriage, and called his daughter home. Only once a year, on the seventh night of the seventh month, is she allowed to visit Dong Yong by flying across the stars of the Milky Way.

# ORANG BUNIAN
## INDONESIA AND MALAYSIA

In Indonesian and Malay folklore, Orang Bunian are elf-like "hidden people." They mainly live in the high mountains and forests, where they eat, sleep, and have families, just like people do. Sometimes they live closer to human beings, but in a parallel world. Orang Bunian are usually harmless, and can even be helpful. But if a baby disappears, or someone goes missing in the forest, it could be because the Orang Bunian have taken them. Only a few people with special sight can see the Orang Bunian. If you are lucky enough to glimpse one, it will look like an old-fashioned human, but with a white, ghostly, foggy appearance.

# MOKSIN TONGBOP
## KOREA

The Moksin Tongbop is a bad-natured imp or fairy creature from Korea. You would not want one in your home, as once they get in, they are said to cause mysterious illnesses. Though they can't enter a house on their own, Moksin Tongbop try to sneak inside by hiding in bundles of firewood, or other wooden objects, when someone carries them indoors.

# THE FAERIE REALM

Where do fairies live? The answer is just about everywhere. Some stories tell of fairy kingdoms hidden in forests, on faraway mountains or remote islands. But many fairies live alongside us, in a "Faerie Realm" that is always there, but invisible to our eyes.

## PARALLEL WORLDS

Iceland's Huldufólk (see page 12) and the Irish Aos Sí (see page 10) are examples of fairies that live among us, but in a parallel, invisible world. The only ones who can see this world and its magical inhabitants are people with special powers, or those who are under a fairy spell.

In some places, fairy doors in the form of a cave, hollow tree, or magical island allow you to pass through into the fairy world, and allow the fairies to enter ours. For example, the fairylike Mimi spirits of Indigenous Australian folklore (see page 33) enter their own world through magical portals in the rocks.

## FARAWAY FAIRYLAND

For some fairies, home is a remote, distant place where humans never normally go. The deep forests of the North, for example, are home to Russia's Leshiye spirits. In Iranian mythology, the Peris (see page 28) live in the faraway land of Jinnestan. Kubera, king of the Yaksha fairies of India, rules from a kingdom in the high Himalayas. And in Māori lands, the goblin-like Ponaturi (see page 33) dwell under the sea, coming ashore only at night.

## IN YOUR HOUSE

Of course, a great many fairies, such as the helpful Brownies (see page 10), the Nisse (see page 12), and the unpleasant Moksin Tongbop (see page 29), live alongside us in our homes. We rarely see them, because they are good at hiding, and can often change shape or become invisible.

## TAKEN BY FAIRIES

In some stories, fairies kidnap humans and carry them off into their own realm. Tam Lin is a fairy knight in an old Scottish legend. He was captured by the Queen of the Fairies, who took him to live in the fairy kingdom of Elfhame, until he was eventually rescued by Janet, his human beloved.

## PLACE NAMES

All over the world, there are places with fairy names, reminding us of the fairies that traditionally live there. Myanmar has a Fairy Island, China has a Fairy Lake, and Italy has a Fairy Mountain. The Isle of Skye in Scotland has beautiful Fairy Pools, and in Turkey, the strangely shaped rock towers of Cappadocia have been named the Fairy Chimneys, after the magical creatures who are said to live inside.

SKYE'S FAIRY POOLS

CAPPADOCIA'S FAIRY CHIMNEYS

## DON'T EAT THE FOOD!

Legends warn that anyone who is abducted by fairies or becomes lost in fairyland may find themselves stuck there forever. But they also offer advice for surviving such an encounter. One way to make sure you don't become enchanted is to avoid eating any food the fairies offer you. That way, you'll remain fully human, and might be rescued.

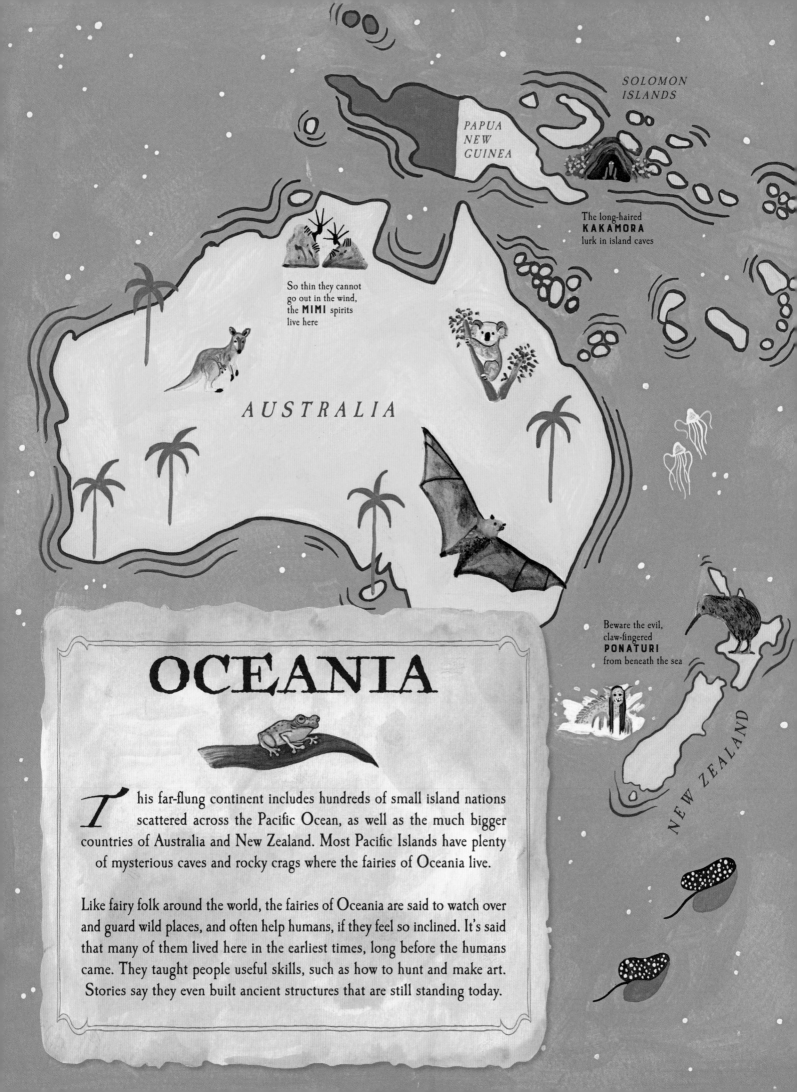

SOLOMON
ISLANDS

PAPUA
NEW
GUINEA

The long-haired
**KAKAMORA**
lurk in island caves

So thin they cannot
go out in the wind,
the **MIMI** spirits
live here

AUSTRALIA

Beware the evil,
claw-fingered
**PONATURI**
from beneath the sea

NEW ZEALAND

# OCEANIA

*T*his far-flung continent includes hundreds of small island nations scattered across the Pacific Ocean, as well as the much bigger countries of Australia and New Zealand. Most Pacific Islands have plenty of mysterious caves and rocky crags where the fairies of Oceania live.

Like fairy folk around the world, the fairies of Oceania are said to watch over and guard wild places, and often help humans, if they feel so inclined. It's said that many of them lived here in the earliest times, long before the humans came. They taught people useful skills, such as how to hunt and make art. Stories say they even built ancient structures that are still standing today.

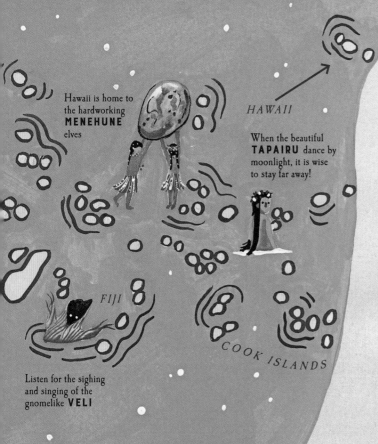

Hawaii is home to the hardworking **MENEHUNE** elves

*HAWAII*

When the beautiful **TAPAIRU** dance by moonlight, it is wise to stay far away!

*FIJI*

*COOK ISLANDS*

Listen for the sighing and singing of the gnomelike **VELI**

# PONATURI
## NEW ZEALAND

New Zealand is home to the Ponaturi, evil sea-fairies of Māori mythology, with red hair and sharp, scary claws. They are said to live under the sea during the day, coming ashore at night to sleep. But they must return before dawn, as sunlight is deadly to them. The Ponaturi recite their magic spells aloud, beating out a rhythm with stolen human bones.

# MIMI
## AUSTRALIA

In Arnhem Land, northern Australia, there are many prehistoric rock paintings of Mimis. These fairylike spirits of Indigenous Australian folklore are said to hide inside rocks, along with animals such as birds, wallabies, and goanna lizards. Their matchstick-thin bodies may break in strong winds, so they only come out when it's not windy. It's said that long ago, when people first came to these lands, the Mimis taught them how to hunt animals, make fires for cooking, and paint on the rocks—which is why there are so many pictures of them left for us to see.

# MENEHUNE
## BUILDING THE FISHPOND

### HAWAII

The Menehune are tiny elf people of Hawaiian folklore. They are excellent builders who work by night and hide in remote forests and valleys by day. It's said they lived in Hawaii long before humans, and that it was the Menehune who built Hawaii's ancient walls, houses, and temples.

One such ancient structure is the famous Menehune Fishpond, on the island of Kauai. Legend tells how, more than a thousand years ago, a princess and her brother asked the Menehune to dam a river and create a fishpond for the royal family. The Menehune agreed, saying the task would take them one night. Their only condition was that no one could watch them at work.

At dusk, the Menehune arrived, and formed a long line, passing lava rocks hand-to-hand to the river. Working at magical speed, they shaped the rocks into the long, thick dam wall as they had promised.

But the curious prince and princess did not keep their promise. They could not resist watching the elves from a ridge on a nearby hill. After a while, they fell asleep, and as dawn broke the Menehune discovered them. Realizing they had been watched, they immediately turned the royal siblings into a pair of rocks, which can still be seen on the ridge to this day.

# FAIRIES OF THE PACIFIC ISLANDS

## KAKAMORA
### SOLOMON ISLANDS

The Kakamora are gnomelike creatures with long hair that grows down to their knees, and long, sharp fingernails. They live in remote limestone caves and come out when it's raining. Kakamora can be dangerous, as they may try to snatch a child or a lost traveler to eat. Luckily, it's easy to scare them off by waving something white—the Kakamora are terrified of anything white and will run away!

## TAPAIRU
### COOK ISLANDS

These beautiful but dangerous female fairies live in a magical pool. It leads to Avaiki, the spirit world, home of their mother, the death goddess Miru. On moonlit nights, the Tapairu emerge from their pool to dance, enticing young human men to dance with them. They then drag their unfortunate victims down through the magical waters to the spirit world, where Miru eats them.

## VELI
### FIJI

Veli are miniature, elf-like creatures that live in hollow trees and rock crevices. They like to keep to themselves, so it's rare to see their big mops of hair and glowing eyes, but according to locals, you can often hear them singing or sighing.

# SIGNS OF FAIRIES

**L**ook carefully when you're exploring the natural world, and you may find all kinds of signs that fairies have been there before you. Of course, some people will tell you there are other explanations for these strange sights. What do you think?

## FAIRY RINGS

A "fairy ring" is a natural ring or circle of mushrooms or toadstools, found on the grass or in a forest. Over many years, fairy rings get bigger, as the network of fungi spreads out underground.

According to folklore, fairy rings are where fairies go to dance at night. It's good luck to see one, or to have one on your farm or in your garden—unless you damage it, of course. If you should see fairies dancing in a fairy ring, do not join in! Those who do are said to have a magic spell cast upon them, forcing them to dance all night long. When they finally return to the human world, they may find that many years have gone by.

# FAIRY LIGHTS

If you walk near a marsh or bog late at night, you might see a spooky, flickering light. These "marsh lights" are caused by gases released from the marsh, glowing as they touch the air. Or are they?

For centuries, people thought marsh lights were glowing fairies, or magical creatures carrying lanterns. They gave them names such as Will-o'-the-Wisp, Jack-o'-Lantern, Pixie lights, and in India, the Chir Batti, or "ghost light." Some stories say these lights reveal where the fairies keep their treasure. But beware: those who follow them are doomed to end up lost in the deep, dangerous marsh.

# LOST PROPERTY

Fairies are well-known for leaving their possessions lying around all over the countryside.
Look carefully, and you might find some of them.

### ELF ARROWS
Are these old stone arrowheads made by Stone Age humans, or are they "elf bolts" used by fairies to shoot people who had annoyed them?

### ELF CUPS
What might look like a pebble with a middle hollowed out by water could actually be an "elf cup."

### FAIRY LOAVES
While some say these are fossilized sea urchins, others know them as fairy loaves.

### FAIRY-SIZED POTTERY
These tiny clay pots are the nests of the Potter wasp, but could also be used by fairies as a water jug.

# A FAIRY GARDEN

The names of these plants suggest the fairies have a few handy uses for them!

### FAIRY DUSTER
This flower is called the Fairy Duster–you can see why!

### FAIRY BELLS
Perhaps the fairies play tunes on these flower bells, or ring them at fairy weddings.

### FAIRY SLIPPERS
These pretty flowers, known as Fairy Slippers, would make perfect fairy footwear.

# NORTH AMERICA

Stretching from the icy Arctic Circle to the tropical Caribbean islands, North America is home to many different peoples, and fairies old and new. Indigenous peoples have been here for thousands of years, and have countless ancient legends of the many types of fairy folk who have shared their lands. Other inhabitants have arrived more recently, in the last few hundred years, only to find that their fairies followed them from Europe, Africa, and Asia.

Though this is a continent with numerous big cities, it also has vast areas of wilderness, and nature of all kinds that needs protecting. There are great plains, forests, and deserts, rolling hills and mighty mountains, swamps, lakes, and seashores. And you could find fairies in any of these places—although, of course, they are often invisible.

CANADA

Don't be unkind, or the **JOGAH** might decide to teach you a lesson!

U S A

Ask an **ALUX** to watch over your farm

MEXICO

In Inuit lands, the **ATLIARUSEK** paddle tiny kayaks

Beware the **GOOD FOLK** when berry-picking

Listen for the drumming of the **YUNWI TSUNSDI** in the forest

Take care when close to a **SILK COTTON TREE!**

## ALUX
### YUCATAN, MEXICO

In Mayan folklore, an Alux is a small, hairless elf. Aluxes guard wild places such as forests and rocks, but they can be tempted to live on a farm instead. To summon an Alux, a farmer makes a little house, and leaves gifts of corn and honey. If an Alux moves in, it will bring good luck and good weather, and scare off intruders by playing tricks on them. After seven years of good luck, the farmer must close up the doors and windows of the miniature house and say goodbye. Otherwise the Alux will turn on its host and bring them bad luck instead!

## YUNWI TSUNSDI
### CHEROKEE NATION, SOUTHEASTERN USA

Yunwi Tsunsdi, meaning "little people," are the fairy folk of the Indigenous Cherokee people of the southeastern USA. They are small, with long hair that reaches almost to the ground. They love music, and when you're in the mountains or forests, it's said you can sometimes hear their drumming. But the Cherokee know better than to follow the sound, as the Yunwi Tsunsdi don't like to be bothered. However, they are kind and helpful. If a child is lost, the Yunwi Tsunsdi will rescue them and bring them home. And remember—if you find something valuable on the ground, such as a necklace or a knife, you must politely ask the Yunwi Tsunsdi before you take it, in case it belongs to them.

## ATLIARUSEK
### NORTHERN CANADA AND GREENLAND

In some Inuit legends, the Atliarusek are said to live in rocks along the seashore, paddle tiny kayaks, and hunt miniature bears no bigger than lemmings. Though small, the Atliarusek are strong and clever, and sometimes help human hunters. However, it's very hard to see them, as if they spot you first, they quickly disappear into the cliffs and coastal caves.

## GOOD FOLK
### NEWFOUNDLAND, EASTERN CANADA

The fairies of Newfoundland, a large island off Canada's eastern coast, are known as the "Good Folk." People picking berries here must take care, as the berries often grow on fairy lands. If the Good Folk are annoyed, they may send strong winds or a thunderstorm. Or even worse, you might be hit with a "fairy blast," leaving you with a strange injury. Just when you think it's starting to heal, string, twigs, and fish bones will fall out of it! To avoid all this, carry bread in your pockets, and wear your hat or jacket inside out. That confuses the fairies, and they'll leave you alone.

## SILK
## COTTON TREE
### CARIBBEAN

In Jamaica and other parts of the Caribbean, the silk cotton tree, or kapok, is a tree of magic and mystery. It's the home of spirits and fairies known as Duppy or Jumbies. Some say that by night, these enchanted trees rise out of the ground and walk around. So take care not to cut one down, and don't plant one near your home!

# JOGAH
## AN IROQUOIS FAIRY TALE
### EASTERN USA AND CANADA

**N**ative American Iroquois folklore includes stories of small fairies called Jogah, living in rocks or underground. They're invisible to most, but it's said that children can see them.

Long ago, so the legend goes, there was a girl who lived with her aunt and uncle. They never hugged her, and only let her eat leftovers. One day, they planned a feast for their friends, but did not invite her. As she sat in a cornfield, sobbing to herself, she suddenly noticed Jogah all around her. The fairies wiped her tears, and put winged moccasins on her feet. She found herself flying up into the air with them.

They came to a large rock, which opened up to let them inside. The girl found herself in a fairy world, where the Jogah made delicious food for her. When she had eaten as much as she could, they set out again for the girl's home, where her aunt and uncle were preparing their feast. "Let's call the wolves," said the Jogah. A pack of huge wolves leapt out of the forest and ran snarling into the house. As the people screamed and ran, the wolves ate up every scrap of the feast.

For many days the girl lived with the Jogah, and was so happy, she wanted to stay with them forever. But the Jogah said, "It's time to go home. Your relatives have learned their lesson." And she found herself in her aunt and uncle's house. When they saw her, they ran and hugged her, and brought her food. From that day on, they treated her like their own daughter, and surrounded her with love.

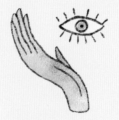 # FAIRY SIGHTINGS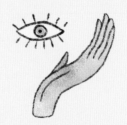

Fairies like to stay hidden, which is easy when you're invisible, too tiny to notice, or live in a mysterious parallel world. We've all heard tales of fairies, but how many people have seen one? Some people are certain they have. Here are some stories of fairy sightings from long ago, and some spotted more recently.

## CHIMNEY ROCK

In 1891, dozens of people reported seeing fairylike beings flying around a mountain at Chimney Rock, North Carolina. At first, a group of children spotted them. When they tried to tell a local man what they'd seen, he thought it was a silly game. But then a woman saw them too, and soon more and more of the villagers went to see the fairies for themselves. They were said to be dressed in white gowns and robes, and resembled humans, except that they could fly.

## FAIRY MUSIC

William Cain was a fiddler (violin player) from the Isle of Man, off the northwest coast of England. He said that he encountered fairies in the early 1900s. Walking in a valley, he saw a strange glass house, lit up from the inside, with magical music coming from it. He remembered the tune, so he could play it on his fiddle when he got home.

# GREEN ELVES

While some see flying, floating fairies, others see elf-like beings dressed in green, as in these three reports . . .

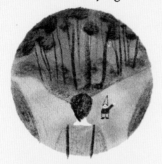

## BERKSHIRE, ENGLAND

A farmer's wife described seeing an elf when she was lost in the Berkshire countryside in 1962. She wasn't sure which path to take, and as she was hesitating, she saw a tiny man right beside her, dressed in green. He told her, "You take that one!"—and then vanished. It was the right path!

## CORNWALL, ENGLAND

Cornwall is famous for its tales of pixies and fellow fairy folk. One real-life report came from a woman who was on a trip there with her daughter. As they walked down a lane, they suddenly saw a little man with pointed ears, wearing a green jacket with a hood. For some reason, they found him terrifying! The daughter screamed, and they ran away as fast as they could.

## NEW HAMPSHIRE, USA

According to a report from 1956, Alfred Horne was cutting Christmas trees in the forest near his house when he realized someone was watching him. Looking up, he saw a little man around 2 feet (60 cm) tall, with green skin and large, floppy ears. Horne decided to try to catch the creature, but it screamed so loudly that he fled in terror.

# PHOTOGRAPHS OF FAIRIES

Have fairies ever been caught on camera? It can be hard to tell . . .

From 1917 to 1920, two cousins in Cottingley, England, amazed the world with five photos of fairies taken in their garden. They were accused of faking the pictures—and many years later they admitted they had cut out pictures of fairies and placed them among the flowers. However, they insisted that they had seen real fairies, too.

Much later, in 2014, a professor named John Hyatt took some photos in Rossendale, England, that seemed to show tiny, glowing, flying fairies. But some say they are simply mayflies, lit up in the evening sun.

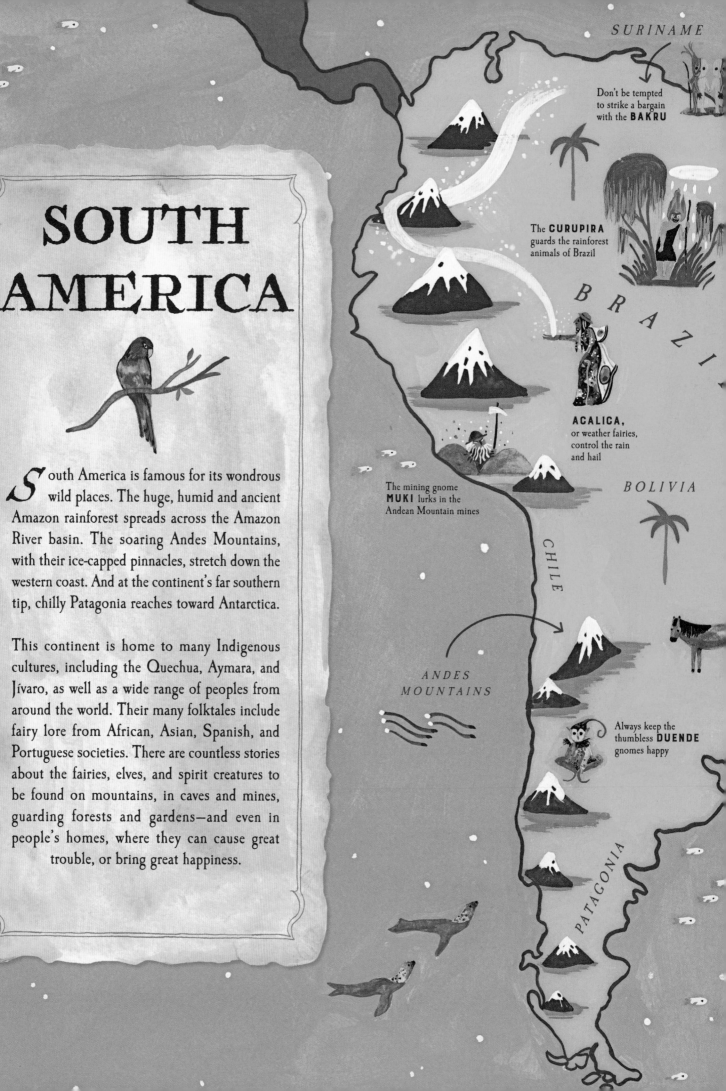

# SOUTH AMERICA

S outh America is famous for its wondrous wild places. The huge, humid and ancient Amazon rainforest spreads across the Amazon River basin. The soaring Andes Mountains, with their ice-capped pinnacles, stretch down the western coast. And at the continent's far southern tip, chilly Patagonia reaches toward Antarctica.

This continent is home to many Indigenous cultures, including the Quechua, Aymara, and Jívaro, as well as a wide range of peoples from around the world. Their many folktales include fairy lore from African, Asian, Spanish, and Portuguese societies. There are countless stories about the fairies, elves, and spirit creatures to be found on mountains, in caves and mines, guarding forests and gardens—and even in people's homes, where they can cause great trouble, or bring great happiness.

*SURINAME*

Don't be tempted to strike a bargain with the **BAKRU**

The **CURUPIRA** guards the rainforest animals of Brazil

*B R A Z I L*

**ACALICA**, or weather fairies, control the rain and hail

*BOLIVIA*

The mining gnome **MUKI** lurks in the Andean Mountain mines

*CHILE*

*ANDES MOUNTAINS*

Always keep the thumbless **DUENDE** gnomes happy

*PATAGONIA*

Home of the mischief-
making, one-legged
**SACI PERERÊ**

## MUKI
### ANDES MOUNTAINS

Metal miners in the Andes are said to share their mines
with the Muki, a bad-tempered mining gnome. A short
creature with a long beard and no neck, his eyes glint
and shine like the silver and copper he seeks. Miners
may spot him trying to steal their tools, or hear him
making strange noises in the tunnels. If they treat him
respectfully, and promise not to tell others about him,
he sometimes helps them find the best places to dig
for metal. But if they blab about their encounter with
the Muki, he might make a tunnel collapse on them.

## CURUPIRA
### BRAZIL

Much of Brazil is covered with tropical rainforest, the home of the forest elf or goblin known as the Curupira. He dresses all in green, his hair looks like fiery flames, and, like a number of fairies around the world, he has backward-facing feet. The Curupira guards and protects forest animals, especially mother animals and their babies. He tolerates those who hunt for food, but if anyone takes more than they need, or goes hunting for fun, the Curupira will be angry. He takes revenge by making trails of backward footprints that lead people astray, leaving them lost in the forest forever.

## DUENDES
### CHILE AND THROUGHOUT SOUTH
### AMERICA

In Chile, and all over South America, you'll hear tales of the Duendes—little gnomelike creatures with tall, pointed hats and, according to some, no thumbs. They live in forests, where they can be helpful to humans, as they will guide anyone who is lost to safety. But they may also invade homes, where they hide in the walls and jump out to scare children, or make objects go missing. If you have Duendes in your house, it's said you can keep them from causing trouble by always giving them the first bite of your food. Simply break a little off and throw it over your shoulder!

## SACI PERERÊ
### BRAZIL

If a cooking pot boils over, milk goes sour, or chickens escape, this mischievous fairy often gets the blame. Though he only has one leg, he can follow people quickly through the forest, whistling loudly to scare them. He can make himself invisible, so his bright red cap can sometimes be seen bobbing around by itself. If you manage to snatch the cap, he must grant you a wish—but this is not as good as it sounds. The cap smells terrible, and you'll never wash the stink away! Get away from the Saci Pererê by crossing running water, or drop a piece of string tied into knots. He'll stop to untangle it and leave you in peace.

# ACALICA
## BOLIVIA

The Acalica are weather fairies of the Bolivian Andes. They live in caves or rocks in the mountaintops, and are usually invisible too, so they are hardly ever seen. However, if you're lost in the mountains, an Acalica might appear to help you find your way. You'll know because it will look like a tiny, wizened old grandpa or grandma fairy. Acalica are said to control the weather, especially rain, hail, and frost, making the difference between a good and a bad harvest. People keep models of these fairies in their homes, to ask for their blessing.

# BAKRU
## SURINAME

The Bakru of Suriname are strange and mysterious fairies. They look like small children, but only half of them is made of flesh, like a human. The other half is wooden. They have large heads with big, black eyes, and always appear in pairs—one male and one female. Some say you can do a deal with the Bakru: they will protect you and bring you wealth, but only if you promise to give them your soul.

# FAIRY GUIDE

If you should ever find yourself in fairy territory, or suspect there may be fairy folk in your house, what should you do? Follow our helpful tips to make sure you keep the fairies happy, and stay safe from fairy magic.

## RESPECT THE NATURAL WORLD

Fairies love nature, and often guard and protect wild places, so always behave yourself when outdoors!

- Don't damage trees, harm animals, or drop litter.
- Take care not to stand on anthills or toadstools—fairies might live there.
- Don't throw stones, in case they hit an invisible fairy.

## BEFRIENDING FAIRIES

Most fairies are harmless as long as you treat them well. Remember . . .

- Fairies love cream, butter, and milk, which can be left out for them overnight.
- Some fairies appreciate it if you also make a little house for them.
- But don't give Brownies new clothes— they'll be offended!

## AWAY WITH THE FAIRIES

- If you see fairies dancing by moonlight, or in a fairy ring, don't let them see you—they might cast a spell on you.
- Definitely don't join in! That could lead to the fairies capturing you and taking you away.
- If fairies do enchant you and lead you away to fairyland, don't eat the food! That way, you can remain fully human and have a chance of escape.